Fish Had a Wish

Fish Had a Wish

Michael Garland

I Like to Read®

HOLIDAY HOUSE • NEW YORK

I Like to Read® books, created by award-winning picture book artists as well as talented newcomers, instill confidence and the joy of reading in new readers.

We want to hear every new reader say, "I like to read!"

_____

Visit our website for flash cards, activities, and more about the series:
www.holidayhouse.com/ILiketoRead
#ILTR

This book has been tested by an educational expert and determined to be a guided reading level E.

I LIKE TO READ is a registered trademark of Holiday House Publishing, Inc.

Copyright © 2012 by Michael Garland
All Rights Reserved
HOLIDAY HOUSE is registered in the U.S. Patent and Trademark Office.
Printed and Bound in October 2018 at Tien Wah Press, Johor Bahru, Johor, Malaysia.
The artwork was created in digi-wood.
www.holidayhouse.com
7 9 10 8 6

Library of Congress Cataloging-in-Publication Data
Garland, Michael, 1952-
Fish had a wish / by Michael Garland. — 1st ed.
p. cm. — (I like to read)
Summary: Fish wishes to be all sorts of animals because each one is special,
then realizes there is something good about being a fish, too.
ISBN 978-0-8234-2394-1 (hardcover)
[1. Wishes—Fiction. 2. Contentment—Fiction. 3. Self-acceptance—Fiction.
4. Fishes—Fiction. 5. Animals—Fiction.] I. Title.
PZ7.G18413Fis 2012
[E]—dc22
2010050124

ISBN 978-0-8234-2757-4 (paperback)

To my mother

Fish had a wish.

"I wish I were a bird!"
said Fish.
"I could fly high up
in the sky."

"I wish I were a turtle.
I could take a nap
on a sunny rock."

"I wish I were a skunk.
I could make a big stink!"

"If I were a bobcat,
I could have spots."

"If I were a bee,
I could buzz
from flower to flower."

"I could be a beaver
and build a big dam."

A mayfly landed on the water.
Fish ate the bug with one bite.
"That was *so* good!"
said Fish.

"It is good to be a fish.
I wish to *stay* a fish.
Yes!
To stay a fish is
what I wish."